THE NATIONAL
FOOTBALL LEAGUE

D0917049

Robert Cooper

DiscoverRoo
An Imprint of Pop!
popbooksonline.com

abdobooks.com

Published by Pop!, a division of ABDO, PO Box 398166,
Minneapolis, Minnesota 55439. Copyright © 2020 by POP,
LLC. International copyrights reserved in all countries. No
part of this book may be reproduced in any form without
written permission from the publisher. Pop!™ is a trademark
and logo of POP, LLC.

Printed in the United States of America, North Mankato,
Minnesota.

052019
092019

THIS BOOK CONTAINS
RECYCLED MATERIALS

Cover Photo: Orlin Wagner/AP Images
Interior Photos: Orlin Wagner/AP Images, 1; Nam Y. Huh/AP
Images, 5, 30; James D. Smith/AP Images, 6–7; Paul Spinelli/
AP Images, 8; Keith Srakocic/AP Images, 9; Pro Football Hall
of Fame/AP Images, 11; AP Images, 12, 21, 29; NFL Photos/
AP Images, 13, 16 (top), 22; David Durochik/AP Images, 14;
Scott Boehm/AP Images, 15, 25; Tony Tomsic/AP Images,
16 (bottom), 31; Vernon Biever/AP Images, 17 (top); Kathy
Willens/AP Images, 17 (bottom); Ryan Kang/AP Images, 19,
28; Gerald Herbert/AP Images, 22–23; Ben Liebenberg/AP
Images, 26; Red Line Editorial, 27

Editor: Nick Rebman
Series Designer: Jake Nordby

Library of Congress Control Number: 2018964849

Publisher's Cataloging-in-Publication Data

Names: Cooper, Robert, author.

Title: The National Football League / by Robert Cooper.

Description: Minneapolis, Minnesota : Pop!, 2020 | Series:
Football in America | Includes online resources and
index.

Identifiers: ISBN 9781532163777 (lib. bdg.) | ISBN
9781644940501 (pbk.) | ISBN 9781532165214 (ebook)

Subjects: LCSH: Football--Juvenile literature. | American
football--Juvenile literature. | National Football
League--Juvenile literature. | Sports franchises--Juvenile
literature.

Classification: DDC 796.33264--dc23

WELCOME TO
DiscoverRoo!

Pop open this book and you'll find QR codes loaded

with information, so you can learn even more!

Scan this code* and others

like it while you read, or visit

the website below to make

this book pop!

popbooksonline.com/national-football-league

*Scanning QR codes requires a web-enabled smart device with a QR code reader app and a camera.

TABLE OF CONTENTS

CHAPTER 1
A SUNDAY TRADITION

More than 60,000 fans fill Soldier Field in Chicago, Illinois. They are all wearing dark blue and orange. Those are the colors of the Chicago Bears. The fans are ready to cheer on their team.

WATCH A VIDEO HERE!

The Chicago Bears are known as the Monsters of the Midway.

The National Football League (NFL)

is the most popular pro sports league

in the United States. Fans wait all year

The Dallas Cowboys can squeeze more than 80,000 fans into their stadium.

for the season to begin. Thousands of

people go to the **stadiums** every week.

Millions more watch at home.

Packers fans are known as cheeseheads.

Each team's fans have **traditions**.

Green Bay Packers fans chant "Go Pack Go." Philadelphia Eagles fans sing "Fly Eagles Fly."

Pittsburgh's stadium becomes a sea of yellow towels during Steelers games.

PASSIONATE FANS

Some groups of fans have names for themselves. They sit in certain areas of the stadium. For example, a group of Cleveland Browns fans sit behind one of the end zones. They call themselves the Dawg Pound.

DID YOU KNOW? Pittsburgh Steelers fans cheer for their team while waving yellow towels.

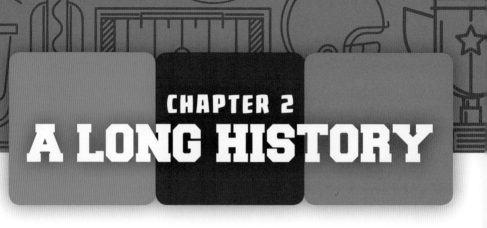

CHAPTER 2
A LONG HISTORY

The NFL began in 1920. The league had 14 teams that year. A few of today's teams date back to the NFL's early years. But most of the league's original teams no longer exist.

LEARN MORE HERE!

The Chicago Bears compete in a game in the early 1920s.

DID YOU KNOW? In 1920, the Akron Pros became the league's first champions.

Over the years, the NFL became more and more popular. New teams joined. And in 1960, a **rival** league started. The American Football League (AFL) had some of the game's most

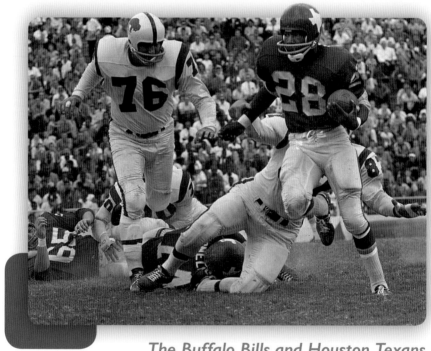

The Buffalo Bills and Houston Texans face off in an AFL game in 1962.

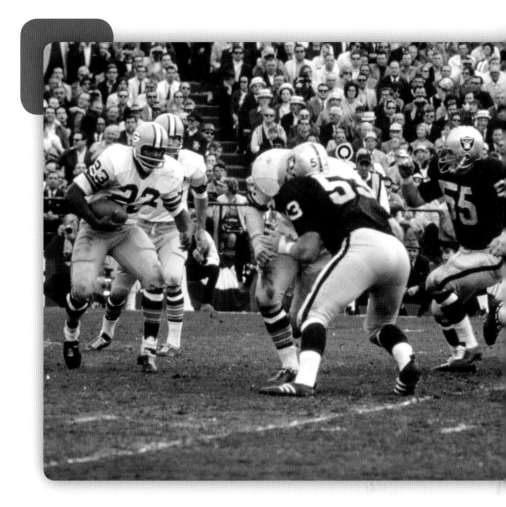

The Green Bay Packers won the first two Super Bowls.

exciting players. Starting in 1967, the NFL

and AFL champions played each other in

the Super Bowl.

The Boston Patriots battle the New York Jets in 1970.

In 1970, the NFL and AFL **merged**.

By this time, the NFL was the most

popular sports league in the United

States. One important reason was that
the NFL had lots of games on TV. Teams
also built nice **stadiums**. These changes
made it easier for fans to watch their
favorite teams.

*Arrowhead Stadium has been home to the
Kansas City Chiefs since 1972.*

TIMELINE

1920

The NFL begins in Canton, Ohio.

1970

The AFL and NFL merge into one league.

1967

In the first Super Bowl, the Green Bay Packers beat the Kansas City Chiefs.

1980

The Pittsburgh Steelers become the first team to win four Super Bowls.

2002

The Houston Texans become the NFL's 32nd team.

2015

More than 114 million people watch the Super Bowl, setting a new **record** for most viewers.

CHAPTER 3
QUARTERBACKS RULE

In today's NFL, the quarterback is the most important player. Nearly every play starts with him. Fans expect the quarterback to lead the team to victory.

COMPLETE AN ACTIVITY HERE!

Carson Wentz of the Philadelphia Eagles attempts a pass against the Washington Redskins.

Quarterbacks weren't always so important. In the NFL's early days, teams ran the ball most of the time. But in the 1960s, quarterbacks such as Johnny Unitas and Joe Namath started passing the ball more often. They helped their teams win many games.

DID YOU KNOW? Joe Namath and the New York Jets won Super Bowl III. They defeated Johnny Unitas and the Baltimore Colts.

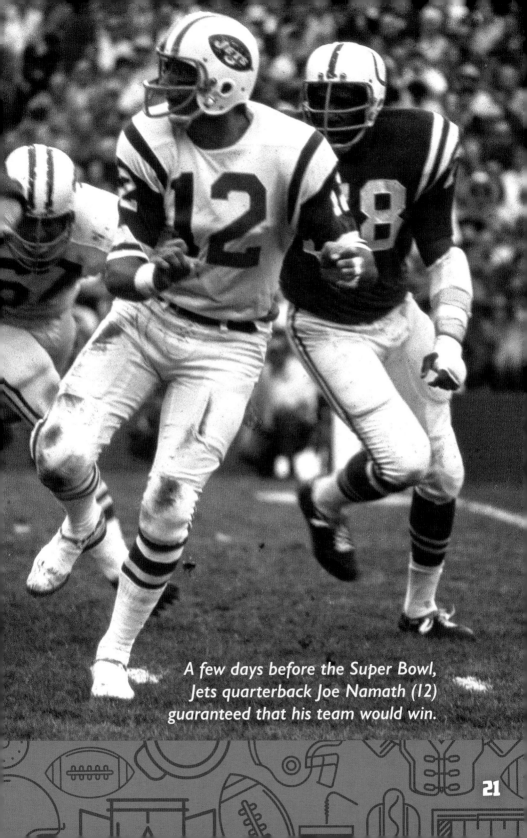

A few days before the Super Bowl, Jets quarterback Joe Namath (12) guaranteed that his team would win.

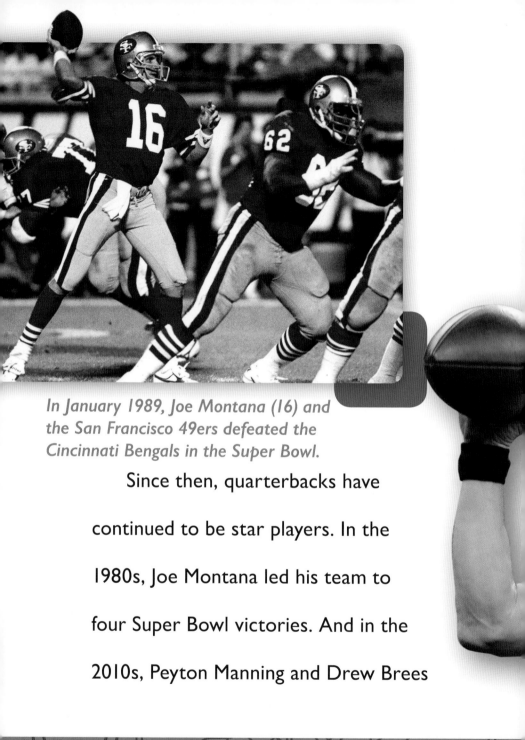

In January 1989, Joe Montana (16) and the San Francisco 49ers defeated the Cincinnati Bengals in the Super Bowl.

Since then, quarterbacks have continued to be star players. In the 1980s, Joe Montana led his team to four Super Bowl victories. And in the 2010s, Peyton Manning and Drew Brees broke many passing **records**. Some quarterbacks, such as Cam Newton, are good at both passing and running. These skills make them even harder to stop.

In 2018, Drew Brees became the NFL's all-time passing leader.

CHAPTER 4
A SUPER GAME

The NFL season comes down to one game each year. The two best teams play each other in the Super Bowl. It's more than a championship game. It's a worldwide event.

LEARN MORE HERE!

The Los Angeles Rams run onto the field before the Super Bowl.

DID YOU KNOW?

The Super Bowl was named after the Super Ball. It was a popular toy in the 1960s.

Thousands of people travel to the Super Bowl **stadium**. And millions more watch the game on TV. Some companies create commercials just for the game. Famous musicians play during the **halftime** show.

Pop star Justin Timberlake performs at the halftime show in February 2018.

SUPER BOWL VIEWERS

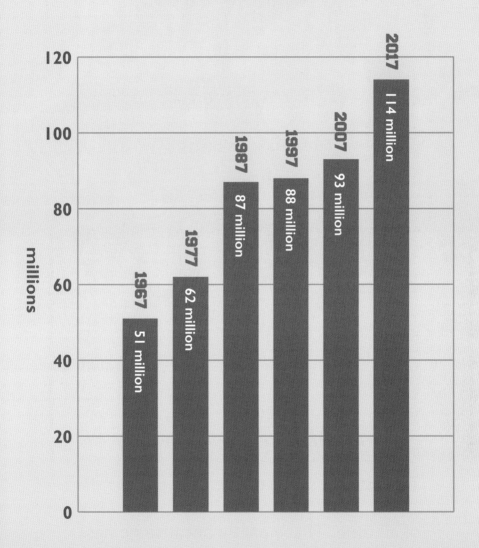

millions

2017 — 114 million
2007 — 93 million
1997 — 88 million
1987 — 87 million
1977 — 62 million
1967 — 51 million

In 2019, Tom Brady won the Super Bowl for the sixth time.

New England Patriots quarterback

Tom Brady is one of the best players

of all time. That's partly because he has

won the Super Bowl so many times. Winning this big game is what it's all about for fans and players. And once the Super Bowl is over, NFL fans can't wait for the next season to begin!

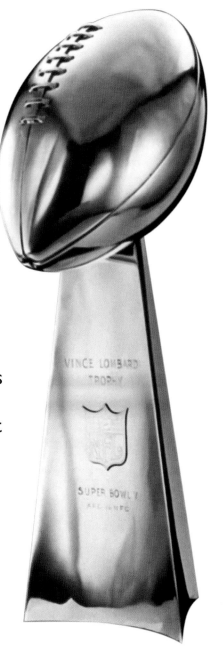

The Super Bowl trophy is named after Vince Lombardi, legendary coach of the Green Bay Packers.

MAKING CONNECTIONS

TEXT-TO-SELF

Have you watched an NFL game? If so, what was your favorite part?

TEXT-TO-TEXT

Have you read a book about another sports league? How is the NFL similar to that league?

TEXT-TO-WORLD

Today, the NFL is the most popular sports league in the United States. Why do you think people prefer football over other sports?

GLOSSARY

halftime – the middle point of the game when the teams take a break.

merge – to join together as one.

record – the best performance of all time in a certain category.

rival – a person, team, or league that has an ongoing competition with another.

stadium – a large building where sports teams play.

tradition – something people do every game to celebrate a team.

INDEX

ONLINE RESOURCES

popbooksonline.com

Scan this code* and others like it while you read, or visit the website below to make this book pop!

popbooksonline.com/national-football-league

*Scanning QR codes requires a web-enabled smart device with a QR code reader app and a camera.